P9-CCH-921

Juliet Fisher and the Foolproof Plan

Also by the Author

Invisible Lissa
The All New Jonah Twist
Josie's Beau
The Best-Laid Plans of Jonah Twist
Ask Me Something Easy

Juliet Fisher and the Foolproof Plan

by Natalie Honeycutt

Bradbury Press • New York

Maxwell Macmillan Canada • Toronto
Maxwell Macmillan International
New York • Oxford • Singapore • Sydney

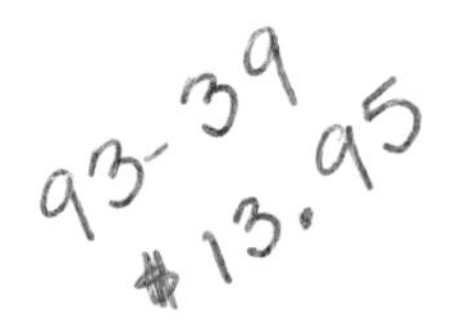

Bradbury Press
Macmillan Publishing Company
866 Third Avenue
New York, NY 10022

Maxwell Macmillan Canada, Inc.
1200 Eglinton Avenue East
Suite 200
Don Mills, Ontario M3C 3N1

Macmillan Publishing Company is part of the Maxwell Communication Group of Companies.
First edition
Printed and bound in the United States of America
10 9 8 7 6 5 4 3 2 1

The text of this book is set in Zapf International Light.

Library of Congress Cataloging-in-Publication Data
Honeycutt, Natalie.
Juliet Fisher and the Foolproof Plan / by Natalie Honeycutt.
p. cm.
Summary: Prim and proper third grader Juliet sets out to serve as a good example for the untidy, enthusiastic Lydia Jane, but Lydia Jane starts to rub off on her instead.
ISBN 0-02-744845-2
[1. Self-perception—Fiction. 2. Popularity—Fiction.
3. Behavior—Fiction.] I. Title.
PZ7.H7467Ju 1992
[Fic]—dc20 91-28119

For Ann Marie,
for rich and seasoned friendship.
With love

Chapter 1

Juliet Fisher unsnapped her rain cap. She slapped it against her knee, spraying droplets of rainwater around the hall of Mills Elementary School. Juliet Fisher was in a bad mood.

The reason for Juliet's bad mood was rain. Juliet knew that California needed rain and lots of it. There had been a long drought. But as Juliet saw it, the job of the rain was to water the trees and grass. It was *not* the job of the rain to water her.

And yet it had. It had soaked the hem of Juliet's dress and the fringes of her hair. It had even dribbled down the back of her neck. And Juliet absolutely hated to get wet.

She walked down the hall to Room 4, the third grade room. She hung her raincoat and hat in her coat cubby. Then she set her lunch box on the shelf above it.

Juliet carried her binder to her half of the double desk she shared with Amber Arlington. Nobody spoke to Juliet as she walked to her desk, but then, she was used to that. Juliet had just one friend in all of Mrs. Lacey's third grade class. The one friend was Jonah Twist and Granville Jones . . . combined.

If Juliet counted them separately, she counted Jonah and Granville as half a friend each. This was because they often seemed to be merely putting up with Juliet. One half friend and one half friend made one whole friend.

Juliet thought that a true, whole friend would not merely put up with her. A true friend would really like her. But there was nobody in Mrs. Lacey's class who really liked Juliet.

Juliet knew the things people said about her. Some kids called her bossy, just because she pointed out the right way to do things. Some kids called her nosy, just because she helped Mrs. Lacey see when someone wasn't working. Some kids called her "The Announcer," just because she mentioned other people's mistakes.

But Juliet knew the truth. She knew she was *motivated.* That's what her mother said she was—motivated. And that was what Juliet needed to be if she was going to grow up to be a doctor. To be a doctor you had to do things right. And you had to start early.

Juliet had started doing things right at age two.

Juliet opened her binder. There were still a few minutes left before the bell would ring. She would use that time to neaten her binder.

Neatening her binder was something Juliet did every morning. She did it because she was motivated. And because she liked it.

She leafed through the papers from front to back. She checked to see that they were all in order by date, oldest in back, newest in front. Then she quickly leafed back through them the other way. This time she checked to see if any needed gummed reinforcements. None did. Just as she finished, Amber Arlington slid into the seat next to Juliet. And a moment later, the bell rang.

Mrs. Lacey started the day with sharing. She did this every morning. Juliet was glad that Mrs. Lacey did things the same way each day. Juliet did not care for surprises.

The first person to share was Sara. She shared about a trip she had taken with her family to the Monterey Bay Aquarium. "Being in the aquarium is just like living in the ocean," Sara said. She didn't say how she knew.

Next Granville shared. He was dressed all

in camouflage fatigues. The last time he'd shared, he had shared a combat helmet. This time he shared a gas mask. "It's in case of attack," he said. "You can buy one of your own at the surplus store." His voice inside the mask was muffled and far away.

Just at the end of sharing, Lydia Jane Bly walked in. Lydia Jane was late nearly every day. Today she was later than usual. At the sight of her, Juliet shuddered. Lydia Jane's curly red hair was plastered with wet to her head. Her electric purple pants were dirt-stained and soaked from the knee down. Her shoes were clotted with mud. Lydia Jane was a mess.

Mrs. Lacey brushed a lock of gray hair back from her forehead and smiled at Lydia Jane. "Lydia Jane, I've been thinking of you," she said. "I've been thinking it might be a good idea to move your seat. How about if you traded seats with Amber?"

Juliet gasped. Trade seats with Amber? That meant Lydia Jane would be sharing

Juliet's double desk! This was a surprise. And not a good one.

"But Mrs. Lacey . . ." Juliet began.

"Now, Juliet," Mrs. Lacey said, "I'm hoping that this arrangement will work better. And I'm sure I can count on your cooperation. Can't I?"

Juliet sank back in her chair. Nobody had to tell her what that meant. It meant that Lydia Jane Bly and Mindy Rufkin had done nothing all day long, every day, except giggle and talk. And Juliet knew whose fault that was.

In second grade, Mindy had been quiet and well behaved. But since sitting next to Lydia Jane, Mindy had turned into a chatterbox. Now she even wore the same neon-colored clothes as Lydia Jane—clothes so bright they hurt a person's eyes. Some days, they both came to school with their hair standing straight up in spikes. They said they used mousse.

Juliet knew that Mrs. Lacey needed her help. She knew Mrs. Lacey wanted Lydia Jane to sit next to someone who could set a good example. And Juliet was the someone who could do it.

Still, Juliet had liked sitting next to Amber Arlington. Amber was shy and tidy, and Juliet barely noticed she was there. Juliet couldn't think of a single thing she might like about sitting next to Lydia Jane Bly.

Lydia Jane arrived with her lunch box, a backpack, an armload of books and papers, a box of tissues, and a handful of pencil stubs. She dropped them all on the desk with a bang and plopped into her seat. She turned to Juliet and grinned.

"You were tardy," Juliet sniffed.

Lydia Jane shrugged. "I'm always tardy," she said.

"Your papers are falling on the floor," Juliet said.

Lydia Jane picked up a handful of the fallen papers and crammed them into her desk. "Guess what I saw on the way to school," she said.

"You should have wiped your feet," Juliet

said. "You tracked mud all over!"

"A newt!" Lydia Jane said. "And not just one, either. A bunch of newts."

"And you should dry your hair," Juliet said. "You'll get sick with wet hair."

"Not me," Lydia Jane said. "I never get sick. Nearly never." She shook her head, hard. Droplets of water whirled off in all directions.

"Hey!" Juliet protested. "You're getting me wet."

"It's just water," Lydia Jane said. "Newts like water. They all came out to enjoy the rain. And they were playing in this muddy stream. Or it *looked* like playing. But maybe it was business. Anyhow, the stream was little, but to a newt I bet it was big. I think it must have been as big as the Sacramento River to a newt. Maybe as big as the Amazon. Do you think that Amazon comes from the word *amazing*?"

Juliet noticed that Mrs. Lacey was writing the spelling words on the chalkboard. She removed a clean piece of paper from her binder. She got a pencil from her desk and wrote her name on the top of the paper. It was time to set a good example.

"Anyhow, I thought about bringing one to school," Lydia Jane said. "But then I thought, what if it's some other newt's brother? Or mother? Or son? And what if it couldn't find its way home when I took it back?"

"Copy each word from the board," Mrs. Lacey said. It was exactly the same thing she said every Monday morning. "Write a short sentence for each word. Don't worry if you don't finish today. You'll have more time on Wednesday."

"And I also thought, well, if I take a newt to school, it might dry out," Lydia Jane continued.

"Shhhh!" Juliet said.

Lydia Jane lowered her voice but went right on. "I mean, maybe they need to stay wet or something. Like a worm can't just take a sunbath on a sidewalk in the hot sun. So if I brought a newt to school, it might get *too* dried out. It might dry out to death. I wonder if there's a word for that? For drying out to death. Like bleeding to death, but different? I mean, I know there is one word that means bleeding to death, because I heard it once. But I forget. So maybe there's a word that means dried out to death. And if a newt . . ."

"Lydia Jane," Juliet said in her most exasperated voice, "you're *supposed* to be doing your spelling."

"Oh," Lydia Jane said. "Yes, I guess . . ." She rummaged in her backpack until she came up with a blank piece of paper. Then she rummaged some more until she came up with a pencil. The paper was frayed. The pencil had been chewed. Lydia Jane chipped at the point of the pencil with her thumbnail. She cleared a space on her desk and smoothed out the paper.

Juliet bent her head over her paper and concentrated on her spelling sentences. She wanted to do a good job. She wanted to write sentences that showed she cared about spelling.

Pail. Leaf. Twenty. Niece. Juliet wrote a sentence for each word. *Island. The island is in the sea.* No, she needed a better sentence than that. *The woman's arms got tired when she paddled the kayak to the island.* There, that would do it.

"Done," Lydia Jane said.

Juliet looked up in surprise. Nobody could have finished so quickly. Juliet still had five sentences to go.

"Lydia Jane, you only wrote three sentences!" Juliet said.

"Yeah, but I used all ten words," Lydia Jane said.

"That's *not* how you're supposed to do it," Juliet said. "You're supposed to write a sentence for each word."

"But that's boring," Lydia Jane said.

"That doesn't matter. . . ."

"And a waste of time."

"But you'll get marked down," Juliet said. "Doesn't Mrs. Lacey mark you down?"

"She gives me a C," Lydia Jane said.

"But you can get an A if you put each word in a sentence. Don't you want an A?"

Lydia Jane shrugged. "C's okay," she said. "A C is average."

"But an A is excellent," Juliet persisted. "Don't you want to be excellent?"

"Not if I have to write more sentences," Lydia Jane said. Then she grinned. "Anyhow, there's nothing wrong with being average. *I'm* average, and there's nothing wrong with that."

Juliet was stunned. All her life she had worked to be excellent. More than excellent, perfect. And here was Lydia Jane, who seemed completely happy to be average. How could anyone be happy being *average*?

No wonder Mrs. Lacey had chosen Juliet to set a good example. No ordinary good example would do. Mrs. Lacey needed someone to set an outstanding example. And Juliet was just the person who could do that.

She turned back to her work. She finished her spelling sentences. She wrote a different sentence for each word. And every sentence was excellent.

After that, and for the rest of the morning, Juliet set good examples. She set her very best examples in everything she did. But by lunchtime, Juliet was tired and discouraged. Lydia Jane, it seemed, did not notice examples, no matter how good.

On rainy days in Mrs. Lacey's class, the kids who brought their lunches from home ate at their desks. Juliet was sorry that Lydia Jane had brought a lunch from home. It would be nice, Juliet thought, if Lydia Jane went far away to eat. It would be nice if she went as far as the cafeteria.

Juliet set her lunch box on her desk and opened the lid. One by one she lifted out the contents and arranged them in front of her. One whole-wheat roll. A thermos of soup. Six slices of orange. Half an apple, no core.

Four whole-wheat fig bars. A small thermos of skimmed milk.

She opened the container of soup. It was lentil. Homemade, and still warm.

Juliet smiled in satisfaction. Another great lunch. That was the best thing about having a mother who was the dietician at Community Hospital. Her mother believed in nutritious food.

"Yuck," Lydia Jane said. She set her lunch box on her side of the desk. "What's that?"

"What's what?" Juliet asked.

"That stuff in the thermos," Lydia Jane said. "It looks gross. Are you going to eat it?"

"It's lentil soup," Juliet said, "and of course I'm going to eat it. It's very healthy."

"That's what parents say whenever they want you to eat something disgusting," Lydia Jane said.

"It's *not* disgusting," Juliet said. "It's delicious." She dipped a spoonful of soup from the mug and blew on it lightly. Then she sipped it down. "Mmmm . . ." she said.

Lydia Jane shrugged. She fished a packet of potato chips from her lunch box and tore it open. She held it out to Juliet. "Want one?" she asked.

"No! Potato chips are very bad for you. They're full of stuff like salt and fat."

"But they taste great," Lydia Jane said cheerfully. She unwrapped a sandwich from her lunch, then popped the top on a soft drink.

Juliet gaped. The sandwich was salami. It was made on white bread. And still sitting in Lydia Jane's lunch box was a doughnut with chocolate icing.

"Lydia Jane!" Juliet exclaimed. "Everything in your lunch is bad for you. You'll die of sugar and saturated fat." Juliet knew about saturated fat. Her mother had told her it was the very worst kind.

"That's dopey," Lydia Jane said. "This is the kind of lunch I always have, and I'm still here."

"But later," Juliet said. "You'll die later.

And even if you don't, your brain can't work with all that sugar. It ruins your concentration. Ask my mother if you don't believe me."

"I don't need to ask your mother," Lydia Jane said. "I can concentrate just fine. Watch if you don't believe me." She picked up her sandwich and took a bite. She chewed very slowly. As she chewed, she stared hard at Juliet.

"What does that prove?" Juliet asked. Anybody could chew a sandwich.

"I'm concentrating," Lydia Jane said between bites. "I'm concentrating on the tip of your nose. I can do that and eat a sandwich at the same time." She took another bite of her sandwich.

"I didn't mean . . ."

"In fact, my concentration is so good I can concentrate on the tip of your nose and tap my foot in time with my chewing. That's three things at once!" She took up a steady tapping with her foot.

"That's ridiculous," Juliet said. "It's not the same as . . ."

"Bet you couldn't do it," Lydia Jane said. "*And* talk at the same time. That's four things! It takes expert concentration." She continued to stare fixedly at Juliet's nose.

Juliet turned back to her soup. She wouldn't talk to Lydia Jane anymore. If Lydia Jane wanted to play a silly game of concentration, she would have to play it alone.

Lydia Jane continued tapping her foot. She chewed her sandwich and stared at Juliet's nose. "This is easy," she said between bites. "When you have great concentration these things are no big deal. In fact, I'll blink, too. That makes five things."

"Everybody blinks!" Juliet said. She had forgotten her resolve not to talk to Lydia Jane.

"But I'm *thinking* about it," Lydia Jane said. "In fact, I'm going to think about my heart beating, too. That makes six!"

Juliet picked up her half apple. She turned sideways in her seat, her back to Lydia Jane.

In a flash, Lydia Jane was out of her seat and in front of Juliet. "No fair," she said. "If I can't see your nose, how can I concentrate on it? I have to do this until the end of lunch." She took another bite from her sandwich and tapped her foot. Crumbs drifted to the floor at her feet.

Juliet opened her mouth. Then, quickly, before the scream came out, she clamped it shut again. She turned back to her lunch and screwed the cap on the thermos of soup. She wished she had never spoken to Lydia Jane in the first place. She wished she had never *heard* of Lydia Jane Bly.

Juliet gathered the remains of her lunch and packed them back in her lunch box. Then she slammed the lid. For Juliet, lunch was over.

Chapter 2

Juliet stomped up the walk to her white clapboard house on Tehema Street. She wanted to slam the door as she went in, but she stopped herself. Her father would be sleeping.

Juliet's father worked as an air traffic controller. He worked on shifts. Right now, he was working a night shift, so he slept in the daytime. There were blackout shades in Juliet's parents' bedroom to keep the light out of her father's eyes. Juliet also knew that her father wore earplugs when he slept. It wasn't so very easy to disturb him. But a slamming door would do it.

Juliet closed the front door quietly. She set her backpack on the bench in the hall, hung her raincoat, and carried her lunch box toward the kitchen. She could smell something cooking even before she got there.

A pot of something spicy smelling was simmering on the stove. Juliet left her lunch box on the table and lifted the lid to the pot on the stove. "Stew?" she said.

"Yes," Mrs. Fisher said. "Rabbit stew. Without the rabbit."

Juliet's mother was covered with flour up to her elbows. She was kneading bread dough on the counter. Her hair was covered with a net. Wearing a hairnet was something she had to do for her job at Community Hospital. She often wore it when she cooked at home as well. She said there was no reason people in her family should want to find hair in their food if people in the hospital didn't.

She bent over and planted a kiss on Juliet's cheek. "Have a good day?" she asked.

"No, I didn't," Juliet said. "I had a horrible day." She opened her lunch box and spread the contents on the table. "In fact, I had the worst day ever in third grade. It may even have been the worst day of my entire life."

"That's impossible," her mother said. "The worst day of your entire life was when Mrs. Lacey assigned you to work on the habitat project with Granville Jones and Jonah Twist. I know because you told me so."

"That wasn't nearly as bad as today," Juliet said. "Besides, that was a long time ago. More than a month. And it turned out okay. And I didn't have to miss my lunch." She got a clean spoon from the utensil drawer and sat down with her soup.

Mrs. Fisher furrowed her brow in concern. "It's not a good idea to skip lunch, dear. Regular meals are very important."

"Tell that to Lydia Jane," Juliet said. "It was her fault. And while you're at it, you might mention that she should eat something besides junk. She has the worst lunches you ever saw."

"Ahhh," said Mrs. Fisher. "So this is about Lydia Jane."

"Yes," Juliet said, "and I don't know how she'll ever learn to behave in class. The only time she pays any attention to me is when I don't want her to."

Juliet polished off the soup, then nibbled at the orange slices. They didn't taste very fresh any longer, but Juliet was too hungry to care.

Her mother flopped and kneaded the bread dough. Little plumes of flour rose from the counter. "I remember when you liked Lydia Jane," Mrs. Fisher said.

"That was all the way back in first grade," Juliet said. "I didn't know any better." She bit into a fig bar.

"Well, there must have been something to

like about her. Maybe you'll remember what it was."

Juliet thought for a moment. She chucked the remaining piece of apple in the garbage. She swept the crumbs from the table and put her empty thermos bottles in the sink.

"I liked her because everyone else did," she said at last. "It wasn't because of Lydia Jane."

"Hmmmm . . ." her mother said. Nothing else, just *hmmmm*.

"Can I punch down the bread dough after it rises?" Juliet asked. Sometimes her mother let her punch down the dough, and something about talking about Lydia Jane made her want to do it today.

"I don't see why not," Mrs. Fisher said. "But it will be a couple of hours."

"That's okay," Juliet said. "I have things to do."

Juliet retrieved her books from the front hall, then headed back through the doorway in the kitchen and up the narrow flight of stairs to her room.

Juliet's was the only room on the second floor of the Fisher house. It had started out as an attic, but Juliet's father had turned it into a bedroom when Juliet was very small.

At the top of the stairs was a polished cherry railing. Dusky peach carpeting covered the floor, and two dormer windows overlooked the backyard. Juliet's desk sat in one dormer, and in the other was a cushioned bench where Juliet often curled up to read.

Juliet could still remember the very day she had moved into her attic room, though she'd been not quite five years old at the time. She'd felt exactly as she imagined a princess might feel, climbing to her room in a castle tower. Sometimes she still felt that way.

Juliet changed from her dress into a yellow sweat suit. She stuffed the dress into a laundry bag and set her shoes side by side on a rack in her closet. She pulled on the soft, suede moccasins her grandmother had sent her from Arizona. Then she got a book from the bookshelf and climbed onto the window seat. It was a book by a man named Hans Christian Andersen, and Juliet had read it before. It had a story in it about a princess and a pea. Juliet could nearly tell the story from memory. She didn't open the book now, but hugged it to her chest and gazed out through the rainy windowpanes.

In her imagination, Juliet erased the fence around her yard. Then she erased all the other fences up and down the alley in back of her house. Then she erased the light poles and sidewalks. Finally she erased the roads and all of the other houses for as far as the eye could see. The only things left were grass and rolling hills and trees.

Juliet was pretty sure that this was the kind of view a princess would have from her tower room.

For several minutes, Juliet enjoyed her imaginary view. Then she thought of Granville Jones. And of Jonah Twist. If she erased her neighborhood, she'd erase them, too.

Jonah and Granville were probably down the street in Granville's tree fort right now. Or maybe the rain was keeping them indoors. But wherever they were, they were most likely hatching plots.

As far as Juliet could tell, Jonah and Granville had done very little *except* hatch plots ever since they had become friends early in the school year. Still, if Juliet erased Jonah and Granville, she might miss them. She put the neighborhood back to the way it was before and opened her book.

It was nearly dark when Juliet's mother called her to come down and punch the bread dough. Juliet rolled up her sleeves and washed and dried her hands. Then she gave the dough several good, hard socks while her mother held the bowl.

"My, you're getting very strong," her mother said.

"I'm in the mood," Juliet said.

Mrs. Fisher turned the bread dough in the

bowl, covered it with a cloth, and dusted the flour from her hands. "I have something that will make your mood brighter," she said. "I picked these up on the way home from work today." She retrieved a small paper bag from the top of the refrigerator and handed it to Juliet.

Juliet peered cautiously inside the bag. There were two packets of cards. Not just cards, invitations. Ten invitations in each packet. *Hooray, A Birthday Party!* they read.

Juliet sank into a chair at the table. "Oh, no . . ." she said.

"Your birthday's coming . . ." her mother said.

"I know," Juliet said.

"And I thought it was time . . ."

"I don't want a party," Juliet said quietly.

". . . that we started to plan," her mother said. "It's only a month away."

"I don't want a party," Juliet said again. She said it slowly and clearly this time, in case her mother hadn't understood.

"Don't be silly," her mother said. "Now I thought that this year it would be nice if . . ."

"I don't want a party!" Juliet said. This time she said it loudly, just in case her mother was losing her hearing.

"Certainly you do," said her mother. "You always have a party."

"Not this year," Juliet said. She folded her arms across her chest.

Mrs. Fisher pulled a chair out from the table. She sat down next to Juliet. "Now, Juliet, darling, be sensible," she said. "I can help you fill these out and we'll be done in no time."

"I *am* being sensible," Juliet said. "I'm being my most sensible ever."

"If you do half and I do half . . ."

"No!" Juliet said. "Anyhow, I don't see what the rush is about. If I *did* want a party—which I *don't*—I would not hand out invitations a whole month early."

She did not bother to add that if she did

want a party she would also want to fill out the invitations herself. Last year, filling out the invitations had been the only part of the birthday party Juliet had truly enjoyed.

"But that's just the point, my dear. Last year not many people came to your party . . ."

"Two," Juliet said. "Two people came."

"Which is why we need to plan ahead," her mother said. "We need to give plenty of notice for a party. If you recall, last year most of your friends had already made other plans."

"That's not why they didn't come!" Juliet shouted. "They didn't come because they don't like me! It had nothing to do with other plans!"

Her mother stared blankly at Juliet for several long seconds. Then she stood up from her seat. "That's the silliest thing I ever heard," she said. "What possible reason could anyone have for not liking you?" And then, without waiting for an answer, she pulled off her apron and left the room.

Juliet picked up the invitations and put them back in the paper sack. She stood on her tiptoes and shoved them back on top of the refrigerator.

She had heard her mother's question. It was a question she had asked herself more than once.

It was just as well, Juliet decided, that her mother had not waited for an answer to her question. Because Juliet didn't have one.

Juliet climbed the narrow stairway back to her room. She sat at her desk and opened her schoolbooks. Mrs. Lacey had given very little homework today. Juliet decided to do it slowly. She wanted to make it last.

Sometimes Juliet wished Mrs. Lacey would give her extra homework, just so she could see Mrs. Lacey's face when she handed it in. Every question would be answered exactly right. Each paper would be sparkling, no smudges anywhere. And at the top, in perfect cursive, would be Juliet's name.

In her mind's eye, Juliet could see Mrs. Lacey as she checked Juliet's homework. She would nod and smile. "More perfect work from Juliet," she would say to herself. Then she would put a bright red A at the top of the paper. And maybe the word *Excellent*, underlined twice. Juliet sighed with pleasure at the thought.

Juliet worked on her homework until dinnertime. Then she and her mother ate no-rabbit stew together. They polished off half a loaf of fresh bread between them. Neither mentioned a birthday party.

Before bed, Juliet packed up her schoolbooks. She laid out her clothes for the morning. Then she turned back the flowered coverlet on her bed and climbed in.

Mr. Fisher came in a few minutes later. His breath smelled of toothpaste. His hair still stood up on one side from sleep.

"What would you do," Juliet asked him, "if you had to sit next to someone who didn't pay attention to anything they were supposed to and who talked about nothing but newts all day?"

Juliet's father chuckled. "I'm afraid that wouldn't work out very well," he said. "Air traffic controllers have to pay strict attention to their work. And they talk about very little except airplanes—at least while they're on the job."

"I'm supposed to help this someone improve," Juliet said. "So far it's not working."

"Have you been at it long?" Mr. Fisher asked.

"One day so far," Juliet said.

"One day isn't a great deal of time," her father said.

"But it was a very *long* day," Juliet said.

Juliet's father pulled the covers snug and tucked them under Juliet's chin. "Helping someone improve is a hard job," he said. "Usually it takes more than time, and the person doing the helping seldom makes herself popular." He put a kiss on the end of Juliet's nose.

"I'm not very popular anyway," Juliet said. Then, to herself she said, Maybe that's how I got the job.

Chapter 3

"*Where's Jonah?" Juliet said to Gran*ville. "He was supposed to be here ten minutes ago."

It was Saturday morning, and Juliet was on Granville's front porch. She and Granville were waiting for Jonah so they could go to Mr. Rosetti's house together.

Mr. Rosetti was an elderly man who lived on Sonora Street, eight doors down from Jonah Twist and around the corner from

Granville Jones. Juliet had first heard of Mr. Rosetti back in October when he'd given Jonah a giant pumpkin he'd grown in his own backyard. Then she heard about him again when he mysteriously disappeared and later turned up right in Community Hospital with a broken hip. Today Juliet would meet Mr. Rosetti for the very first time. For the occasion, she had worn patent-leather shoes and her second-best dress.

Granville had on a San Francisco Giants' T-shirt and desert camouflage pants. Over his shoulder was hung a box on a strap. Inside the box was his gas mask. Juliet wished Granville had worn something else. His clothes often made her nervous.

Granville dangled a piece of yarn in front of a medium-sized kitten. The kitten was black and white. The kitten used to belong to Granville, but now it belonged to Mr. Rosetti. Granville had been taking care of it for him.

"Jonah's late," Granville said.

"He's always late," Juliet said. She jammed her fists into the pockets of her sweater.

"He's not *always* late," Granville said. "He's late about half the time. Once he was early."

"It's bad manners to be late," Juliet said.

"I don't think Mr. Rosetti will care if we're late," Granville said. The kitten swiped at the piece of yarn, then leaped in the air.

"It's still bad manners, whether he cares or not," Juliet said sharply.

"What's bugging you?" Granville asked. "You've been grumpy ever since you got here. Come to think of it, you've been grumpy for days. Don't you *want* to meet Mr. Rosetti?"

"It's not Mr. Rosetti," Juliet said. "It's other people. Lydia Jane Bly, for one. And my mother, for two."

"You have to be careful with mothers," Granville said. "They can mess up lots of plans."

"Sometimes they *make* plans," Juliet said. "My mother is making plans right this minute. She's planning my birthday party, even though I don't want one."

Granville picked up the kitten and tickled its tummy. "That's cuckoo," he said. "I never heard of anyone who didn't want a party. I'd have a birthday party every week if I could. Think of all the presents!"

"You don't get presents if people don't come," Juliet said.

"True . . ." Granville said.

"And nobody would come to *my* party if it were the last birthday party on earth," Juliet said. "I'm unpopular."

Granville cradled the kitten in his arms and leaned on the porch rail. He seemed to be thinking. "I'd come," he said at last, "but I don't go to girls' birthday parties."

"See?" Juliet said. She sank down on the top step of Granville's porch and rested her head in her hands.

Granville came and sat beside her. "I could give you a present, though," he said. "I still have one kitten left besides this one.

I could give you a kitten for your birthday."

"Can't," Juliet said. "I'm allergic. Anyhow, it's not the presents. It's being unpopular that's the trouble. It means I'll have a party without any guests. And it's also how come I'm stuck sitting with Lydia Jane Bly."

Granville thought about this. He could see how being unpopular would make a birthday party tricky. But he didn't see how it could land Lydia Jane next to Juliet—especially since Lydia Jane *was* popular. "I don't get it," he said at last. The kitten rolled over and slid off his lap. It bounded across the lawn and pounced on a blade of grass.

"It's simple," Juliet said. She explained how Mrs. Lacey wanted her to set a good example for Lydia Jane. And she told how Lydia Jane had ignored Juliet's best examples for a whole week.

"It's hard work getting someone to improve," Juliet said. "And the person who's stuck with the job ends up unpopular. My dad told me that."

Granville cleared his throat. He looked off in the distance, then down at his feet. Then he looked off in the distance and cleared his throat again.

"Juliet . . ." Granville said. "Ahem . . . it's just . . . well . . . you were *already* unpopular."

Juliet stood up and stomped her foot. "Granville Jones!" she said. "You're not listening! I *know* I'm unpopular. And so does everyone else. That's why Mrs. Lacey gave me the job. If I'm already unpopular I can't get *more* unpopular, can I?"

"Well, you *could* . . ." Granville said.

"And this saves a popular person from having to do a job that would make her unpopular. Don't you *see*?"

Granville scratched his head. He wasn't sure he saw. But he didn't want to argue with Juliet. "I was unpopular at my old school," he said. "But it wasn't this much trouble."

Juliet sighed and stood up. "That's because you didn't have Lydia Jane at your old school," she said. "Lydia Jane is the worst part of the trouble."

Just then, Jonah came careening around the corner on his bike. He rolled across Mr. Rosetti's lawn and then up Granville's lawn to the steps. "Sorry I'm late," he said as he got off. "I thought for a minute maybe you went without me."

"No way," Granville said. "This kitten is a present we both gave Mr. Rosetti. We have to take it to him together."

"It's rude to be late," Juliet sniffed. "Plus, you're not supposed to ride bikes on people's lawns."

"*I* am," Jonah said cheerfully. "Mr. Rosetti told me to."

Juliet blinked. She'd heard that Mr. Rosetti was special. But she'd thought it meant special like magic. Now she wondered if it meant special like strange. She hoped not.

More likely this was one of Jonah's misunderstandings. Jonah often got things mixed up. If he thought Mr. Rosetti wanted him to ride on his lawn, it was probably another of Jonah's mistakes.

Granville rolled the yarn in a ball and stuffed it in his pocket. "All set," he said. He struck off across the lawn with the kitten in his arms. Jonah followed behind.

Juliet smoothed her dress and walked down Granville's front walk. She turned left at the sidewalk and walked to the corner. She turned left at the corner and walked to Mr. Rosetti's front walk. Then she turned left at Mr. Rosetti's front walk and walked up to his porch.

Jonah and Granville were already there. So was Mr. Rosetti, standing in the open doorway.

"Where'd you go?" Granville asked.

"I walked on the sidewalk," Juliet said. "That's what it's *for*."

"This is Mr. Rosetti," Jonah said. He said it with pride, like he'd just discovered America.

Mr. Rosetti was a big man with bushy eyebrows and thick white hair. Juliet was suddenly confused. She couldn't remember whether she was supposed to shake hands or curtsy. She clutched the edges of her skirt as Mr. Rosetti stuck out a brown-speckled hand. In his other hand, he held a four-footed cane.

"You must be Juliet," he said. "Welcome."

Juliet shook his hand. "Thank you," she said. She was glad she hadn't curtsied.

"I met your mother while I was in the hospital. She told me a lot about you. You're planning to be a doctor, I hear."

"A brain surgeon," Juliet said. "I'm motivated."

"Is that so?" Mr. Rosetti said. "Well, please come in." He stood slightly aside in the doorway.

Granville and Jonah marched right through. Juliet followed behind.

"You're supposed to wait," she hissed at Granville. "Ladies first."

"What's that?" Mr. Rosetti said. "I'm afraid I'll have to ask you to speak up, Juliet. I'm somewhat hard of hearing, you see, so if you don't speak up I sometimes miss things."

A flush crept up Juliet's cheeks. She hadn't meant Mr. Rosetti to hear. But then, it was rude to whisper. "I just told him, *ladies first*," she said. "Sometimes Granville doesn't mind his manners."

"Ahhh," Mr. Rosetti said.

"What manners?" Granville asked. "Here's your kitten, Mr. Rosetti. It's getting pretty big. It'll be a cat in a few months."

"Ahhhhh," Mr. Rosetti said again. Somehow it sounded like a completely different word.

"I've been looking forward to this day," he said. "Ever since you boys smuggled this kitten into the hospital, I've been imagining how much I'd enjoy having it in the house. I'm only sorry I had to delay so long in accepting your gift."

Jonah said, "I asked my mother to tell your sister Violet a kitten wouldn't be any trouble. Since they got to be friends and all. And since *my* kitten is no trouble. Well, hardly any trouble. But I guess your sister wouldn't listen."

Juliet wondered if Mr. Rosetti could understand what Jonah was saying. He often said things in a way that was hard to sort out.

"My sister Violet rarely listens to anyone," Mr. Rosetti said. "She much prefers to give orders." He settled into an upholstered chair and held his hands out for the kitten. As soon as it got on Mr. Rosetti's lap, the kitten curled up in a ball to sleep.

"Of course, when she explained to me that she was afraid one of us would trip over the kitten, I could see her point," Mr. Rosetti said. "I found myself imagining that Violet tripped over the kitten and broke *her* hip. If that had happened, I'd have been stuck with Violet for six weeks, instead of the two weeks she stayed. I was a little afraid to take the chance." Then Mr. Rosetti chuckled.

"But aren't you afraid you'll trip and break your other hip?" Juliet asked. She hated to bring it up, but it sounded to her like Mr. Rosetti's sister might be right.

"Not a bit," Mr. Rosetti said. He stroked the sleeping kitten lightly on the back. "Not one bit."

"I'll get some juice," Jonah said.

"Jonah!" Juliet said. "You're supposed to wait until it's offered!"

"Juice is a very good idea," Mr. Rosetti said. "I've set some out on the kitchen counter already. And there are four glasses. If you can manage, I'd appreciate it if you'd bring it all in here. This cane keeps me from carrying more than one thing at a time, or I'd have done it myself."

"Sure thing," Jonah said.

"Want me to help?" Granville asked. His voice was muffled. He was wearing his gas mask.

"Granville, take that off!" Juliet said. "It's exactly the same as wearing a hat in the house. You're not supposed to wear a hat in the house!"

"It's not the same," Granville said. "A hat goes on your head. A gas mask goes on your face. It's completely different."

Mr. Rosetti started to chuckle.

Juliet stomped her foot. "You're impossible," she said to Granville. "You do things wrong on purpose."

"Ha, ha, ha," Mr. Rosetti laughed. "Juliet, you know what? You're beginning to remind me of someone. Granville," he said, "leave it on. I like the effect. And while you're helping Jonah with that juice, you'd better look around the kitchen and see if you can find a straw. Otherwise, I'm afraid you'll go thirsty. Ho, ho, ho."

"I'll help, too," Juliet said. Maybe if she got out to the kitchen with Granville, she could convince him to take that stupid gas mask off.

"Oh, no," Mr. Rosetti said. "I think you should sit right down on the sofa and relax." Then he shook his head. He started to laugh again. "Just like her," he said to himself.

"Har, har, har. Never saw anything like it."

Juliet sat on the couch and looked anxiously at Mr. Rosetti. She couldn't tell who he was talking to, or what he thought was so funny. Maybe he was talking to the kitten. That might be it.

The sleeping kitten rode up and down on Mr. Rosetti's lap as he chuckled. It never even lifted its head. Juliet thought Mr. Rosetti looked like a nice old man who liked cats. She hoped he wasn't crazy. She'd heard that crazy people talked to themselves and laughed at nothing.

Jonah and Granville returned with four glasses of apple juice and one straw.

"Have you picked out a name for your kitten yet?" Jonah asked.

"Not yet," Mr. Rosetti said. "Most of my life I kept a dog, you see. This is my very first cat, and I thought I should live with it a while before I named it. So I don't give it a dog's name by accident."

"Good thinking," Jonah said. "My cat is

named Mrs. Einstein." He'd told that to Mr. Rosetti once before, but he felt like saying it again.

"My cat is named Mulberry," Granville said.

"What about you?" Mr. Rosetti said to Juliet. "Do you have a cat, too?"

"No," said Juliet. "I'm allergic. I can't have animals with fur or feathers. And I hate reptiles. So I don't have any pets." As she said this, Juliet felt a small lump in her throat. She'd never felt sorry about not having a pet before, but somehow she did now. She took a sip of juice to wash down the lump.

"That's a shame," Mr. Rosetti said. He wasn't laughing now. "I'm very sorry to hear that, Juliet."

Later, as they left, Mr. Rosetti stood in the doorway and waved. The kitten stood next to him. It did not try to leave. It seemed already to understand that it had a new home.

"Remember to cut across this lawn on your bikes," Mr. Rosetti called.

"We will!" Jonah and Granville called back.

Juliet stood on the sidewalk and stared at Mr. Rosetti. He had invited them each to come back. Juliet wasn't sure she wanted to go back. She thought she'd wait a while before she made up her mind.

"We're going to the tree fort," Jonah said to Juliet. "You can come if you want."

"In my good dress?" Juliet asked.

"So go home and change," Granville said.

"Not unless you take off that silly gas mask," Juliet said.

Granville shrugged. "Juliet's in a bad mood," he said to Jonah. "She doesn't like sitting with Lydia Jane Bly in school."

"Why not?" Jonah asked. "Lydia Jane is interesting. She was telling me about these newts."

"Interesting to you, maybe," Juliet said. "To me she's just trouble."

Granville explained. "Mrs. Lacey put Lydia Jane there for punishment or something," he said.

Jonah looked puzzled. "What did you do

wrong?" he asked. It was hard to imagine Juliet misbehaving in class. He'd certainly never *seen* her misbehave.

"Not *me*," Juliet said with annoyance. Leave it to Jonah to mix things up. "It's Lydia Jane who's always doing things wrong."

"Oh," Jonah said. Now he understood. "I guess it would be a pretty bad punishment to sit next to you."

Juliet turned on her heel and walked away. Jonah and Granville called after her, but she did not answer. She walked all the way home without once looking back. When she got in her house she slammed the door.

Chapter 4

Maybe I'll just quit, Juliet said to herself on Wednesday afternoon. Maybe I'll just quit school and quit everything. I'll pack my suitcase and move to Grandma's in Flagstaff.

Juliet was at her desk in Mrs. Lacey's room. She was trying to work on the third part of her habitat studies. Every afternoon this week, Mrs. Lacey had given them time to work on the study.

"It's to be a report on *human* habitats this time," Mrs. Lacey had said. "I want you to make a booklet. It can be about any habitat that you think would be good for human beings.

"It can be about a kind of human habitat that already exists some place in this world. Or it can be a habitat you dream up.

"You can draw pictures, you can write poems, you can cut out photos from magazines. Use your imaginations."

"Can it be about a human habitat that *isn't* good?" Kenny Ota asked.

"Yes," Mrs. Lacey said, "just so long as you tell me how it could be better."

"Can it be about more than one habitat?" Sara asked.

"Yes," Mrs. Lacey said. "Or it can be about just one part of a very large habitat."

"Can it be a habitat for kids?" Granville asked.

"Yes," Mrs. Lacey said. "It can be for people like you, or it can be for people who are nothing at all like you. You choose."

Mrs. Lacey set a large collection of magazines on the shelf by the windows. There were news magazines and history magazines and architecture magazines and catalogs. There were travel magazines and science magazines. Some were old and were missing pages. Others were nearly new. There must have been two hundred magazines. Juliet wondered whether Mrs. Lacey had collected them from friends, or if she had saved them up all her life.

With so much to choose from, Juliet felt uncertain. She liked assignments where the rules were very strict. That way she knew exactly what to do to get an A. Without many rules, it was hard to decide what was right.

On Monday, Juliet was taken with some photos of containers. She cut out pictures of shelves with compartments. She cut out other pictures of plastic boxes with snap-lock lids. All of these things looked like good ways to organize a habitat. No habitat could be good, Juliet reasoned, if it was disorganized.

Using rubber cement, Juliet carefully glued these pictures onto colored paper. She wrote captions and glued them under each picture.

Use these shelves to keep your habitat tidy, said one.

Save important things in boxes, said another.

Lydia Jane, in her seat next to Juliet, cut out pictures of trees. She glued them onto pieces of plain white paper. Some pictures she glued on crooked. Others were wrinkled. Rubber cement oozed around the edges of the pictures.

"Habitats need to have trees," Lydia Jane said. "Trees make oxygen. Without oxygen, nothing can breathe. Did you know that some newts don't have lungs? They can breathe through their skin. I found that out. Of course, they don't have noses, either. What use is a nose to a newt if it doesn't have lungs?"

Lydia Jane pinched her nostrils shut with

one hand. "I can still breathe without a nose," she said. "I can breathe through my mouth. But if I close my mouth, too, then I can't breathe. I just get dizzy. Watch." She closed her mouth.

"Don't do that," Juliet said. "You might faint."

"Mmmmmm mmmmmm," Lydia Jane said. "Mmmm mmmmmm mm!"

"Stop it!" Juliet said. "Anyhow, you have rubber cement on your hand. You're getting it all over your nose."

Lydia Jane crossed her eyes, then she let go of her nose. She wiped her nose on her sleeve. "Newts have it easy," she said. "You try breathing through your skin, see how it works."

"Mrs. Lacey wants us to work on this habitat study," Juliet said firmly. "She didn't say we could talk. And she would not like it if we fainted in class!"

Really, Juliet didn't know why she had spoken to Lydia Jane in the first place. Every day the same thing happened. Juliet would swear to herself not to speak one word to Lydia Jane. Then the next thing she knew, she was talking. Lydia Jane sure was making it hard to set a good example.

On Tuesday, Juliet cut out pictures of cleaning supplies. Then she cut out dead bolts and smoke alarms. A good habitat should be clean, she reasoned. It should also have safety features.

Lydia Jane was drawing a picture with colored pencils. It looked like a picture of worms. Or maybe they were bugs. Or maybe they were space creatures.

"These are bacteria," Lydia Jane said. "My habitat is going to have lots of bacteria."

"Ugh!" Juliet said. "Bacteria are germs."

"They're not *only* germs," Lydia Jane said. "They're good for lots of things. We come from bacteria. They were the first things alive in this world. And if we didn't have them, then Earth would have too much carbon dioxide. And it would be too hot to live here.

Just like Venus. Venus needs a bunch of bacteria."

"You're making this up," Juliet said. "In the hospital they have to get rid of bacteria all the time. Germs make people sick."

"Okay," Lydia Jane said. "*You* have a habitat without bacteria, then. But you won't have people. Try it and see."

Juliet looked at Lydia Jane's drawing of bacteria. She looked at her own pictures of cleansers and alarms. Suddenly she felt confused about the habitat study. She wished Mrs. Lacey had given better instructions.

"Can't you work without talking?" she said to Lydia Jane. She gathered her pictures in a stack and stuck them in her desk. She did not glue them to colored paper.

On Wednesday afternoon, Juliet found a picture of cliff dwellings in Arizona. The cliff dwellings were places where Indians had once lived, long before anyone could remember. Juliet recognized the pictures because they were in Canyon de Chelly. Her grandmother had taken her to Canyon de Chelly two summers ago. It struck Juliet that a cliff dwelling was an odd place to live. It would not be a comfortable habitat for people, she thought.

Lydia Jane had cut out a picture of a fat woman in a long dress. The woman's mouth was open. Lydia Jane slathered glue on a sheet of paper. Then she slapped the picture into place. Underneath, on a sloping line, she wrote, *The Singing Teecher*.

"You spelled 'teacher' wrong," Juliet said.

"No, I didn't," Lydia Jane said.

"Yes, you did," Juliet said. "It's *T-E-A*. Look it up if you don't believe me."

"Well, it's not *much* wrong," Lydia Jane said. "You read it, didn't you?"

"Wrong's wrong!" Juliet spluttered. "It's *completely* wrong." Really, she didn't know what was the *matter* with Lydia Jane. "Besides," she went on, "this booklet is supposed to be about habitats, not the people *in* them. Didn't you listen to the directions?"

"The singing teacher is part of the habitat," Lydia Jane said. "She's what makes it peaceful. I'm dreaming up a peaceful habitat."

"Singing teachers don't make peace," Juliet said. "Peace comes from . . ." She hesitated. Just offhand, Juliet wasn't sure where peace came from.

"From singing teachers!" Lydia Jane supplied. "See, there will be lots of teachers and they will teach everyone how to sing. And everyone will sing every day. And that makes peace, because nobody can fight and sing at the same time."

"That won't work," Juliet said. "It doesn't even make sense. Really, Lydia Jane, I don't know how you're ever going to improve if you don't even try."

Lydia Jane picked at a smear of dried rubber cement. She rolled it between her fingers. "Juliet?" she asked. "Do I make you mad?"

"Yes," Juliet said. "You make me very mad. You're also driving me crazy."

"Then try singing," said Lydia Jane.

Juliet suddenly understood why Indians would want to live in caves on the side of a canyon. If Juliet lived in a cliff dwelling she would not have to sit next to Lydia Jane. Lydia Jane could never even *find* her. She picked up her scissors and carefully cut out the picture of Canyon de Chelly.

On the way home that day, Juliet thought about moving to her grandmother's house. Or farther. As far away as a canyon, for instance.

Nobody would mind, she told herself. The kids at school might even be happy. And her mother was so busy planning a birthday party that Juliet didn't want that she'd probably never even see Juliet leave.

Just yesterday, Juliet's mother had brought home party hats. They were bright blue hats with metallic stars painted all around. They reminded Juliet of something a wizard would wear.

Thinking of wizards reminded Juliet of

castles. Castles reminded Juliet of her room.

"I'd miss my room," she said out loud to no one. A cliff dwelling probably wouldn't have peach carpeting. Or a cushioned window seat.

"Yo," came a voice.

Juliet stopped walking. She was on Manzanita Street, a block from her house on Tehema Street. She looked up the street and down. Then down the street and up. She didn't see anyone.

"Yo, Juliet," came the voice again.

Juliet turned in a circle, looking.

"Up here," said the voice. "Over your head."

Juliet craned her head back and looked up. Over her head were the spreading brown branches of a liquidambar tree. Nothing else. Then she saw a movement. Some sort of green lump along one of the lower branches.

Granville's face appeared in the Y of the branch. "Surprised?" he grinned.

"What are you doing up there?" Juliet said.

"You'd better get down before you fall."

Granville backed down the branch. Then he did a slow, hanging somersault and landed on the parking strip by Juliet.

"I was camouflaged," Granville said. "Bet you were surprised."

"The tree has no leaves yet," Juliet pointed out. "It's all brown. Your camouflage clothes are green. Anyone could have seen you."

"Well, my desert camouflage is brown," Granville said. "But it's in the wash. Next time I'll wear it, and you'll really be surprised."

"I don't want to be surprised," Juliet said. "I hate surprises."

Granville bent down and picked up a spiky round seedpod that had fallen from the liquidambar tree. He tossed it in the air and caught it with one hand. "Jeez, Juliet," he said. "You don't like anything. You don't like birthday parties and you don't like Lydia Jane and you don't like surprises."

"I like some things," Juliet sniffed.

"Such as?" Granville asked.

Juliet considered. "My room," she said. "I was on my way there when you dropped out of that tree."

"Well . . ." Granville said. There was a twinkle in the corner of his eye. "If you want to come to our tree fort on Saturday, Jonah and I have something else you might like."

"What's that?" Juliet asked.

Granville opened a snap pocket on the leg of his camouflage pants. He dropped in the seedpod. "A plan," he said. "Jonah and I have a plan."

Chapter 5

Early on Saturday morning, the scent of warm bran muffins drifted out of the Fisher kitchen and up the stairs to Juliet's room. Juliet smelled the muffins before she even opened her eyes. Her mother had put cinnamon in them, Juliet could tell.

Juliet lay in bed and thought about her day. She was curious to hear Jonah and Granville's plan. But she had her doubts about going to the tree fort. Juliet had never climbed a tree.

She was pretty sure she'd fall if she tried. Or she'd get stuck up there. The fire department would have to come and carry her down. Maybe today was a good day to stay home.

Downstairs Juliet could hear her parents. They were quarreling. The only time Juliet's parents quarreled was on Saturday mornings. And the quarrel was always the same.

"You'll kill yourself eating eggs," said Juliet's mother.

"It's not eggs, it's *egg*. Just one egg," said her father.

"But it's still full of cholesterol," Mrs. Fisher said.

"It's one soft-boiled egg," Mr. Fisher said. "Not even cooked in butter. Just one, plain, simple, soft-boiled egg."

"You might have some respect for your arteries," Mrs. Fisher said. Her voice was rising. "I'll never understand how you can go on eating something that you know will clog them up. If you worked in a hospital and saw the heart patients . . ."

"One lonely egg!" Mr. Fisher shouted. "All week long I wait for Saturday so I can eat this one lonely egg. When I was growing up I had two eggs every morning. Cooked in butter. With milk. Cholesterol and saturated fat by the bucket! And now you can't let me enjoy one measly soft-boiled egg. Do I have to move out so I can eat an egg in peace?"

Something clattered sharply in the kitchen sink. "Eat your egg," Mrs. Fisher said. "It's your funeral."

Juliet sighed. The quarrel was over. Now her parents would be friends again. And they would not have another quarrel until next Saturday.

Juliet pushed back the flowered coverlet and got out of bed. She took her robe from the closet and put it on. She slipped the suede moccasins on her feet. Then she padded down the stairs.

Juliet's mother stood wiping crumbs from the kitchen counter. Her father slurped at his egg.

"How's your project coming, sweetheart?" he asked.

"Not great," Juliet replied. "I can't come up with a good habitat yet. Mrs. Lacey didn't give many instructions." She took her place at the table and reached for a bran muffin. A glass of orange juice was already waiting by her plate.

"I was thinking of that other project," her father said. "The one with the girl. What's her name?"

"Oh. Lydia Jane, you mean," said Juliet.

"That's the one."

"Worse," Juliet said. "Lydia Jane acts just the same as she always did. She's stuck or something."

"I was afraid of that," her father said.

Juliet spread butter substitute on her muffin. "At least I'm not becoming more unpopular," she said. "There's no chance of that."

Her mother carried a cup of dandelion tea to the table and sat down. "I do wish you'd stop this nonsense about other children not liking you," she said. "We're going to get those invitations in the mail right after breakfast. Then you'll see."

Oh, no, Juliet thought. "All I want to do is eat this muffin," she said. "Do I have to leave home so I can eat my breakfast in peace?"

"Juliet!" her mother said.

Juliet groaned. She rubbed her suede moccasins together. She thought about Arizona. She wondered whether it would be quicker to go by bus or train.

Then she had another thought. "I can't, anyway," she said. "I'm going to Granville's tree fort. He and Jonah invited me. In fact, I need to hurry. I need to go there right after breakfast."

Juliet ate two muffins with butter substitute. She drank two glasses of orange juice. Then she went upstairs and changed into her yellow sweat suit.

Yellow, Juliet thought, was a good color.

It was a color everyone could see. It would be a good color to have on when the fire department came to get her out of Granville's tree.

Juliet went through her backyard gate to the alley behind her house. The alley ran between Tehema Street, where Juliet lived, and Sonora Street, where Jonah and Mr. Rosetti lived. It ended at Manzanita Street, where Granville lived.

Juliet walked down the alley, between the high fences on both sides. It was hard to tell whose house was whose from the back. Juliet thought the alley should have house numbers like the streets did. That way people could visit and not get mixed up.

An overnight rain had left puddles in the alley. Juliet walked carefully around them. At the end of the alley she spotted the huge California live oak in Granville's yard. And she saw the weathered slats that formed the sides of the tree fort.

She pushed open the gate to Granville's

yard. *Clank, clankety, bong, clank!* Juliet jumped.

"Intruder alert! Intruder alert!" Granville yelled.

"Arm the rocket launchers!" Jonah yelled. "Check the radar!"

Dented pans and empty soda cans lay scattered at Juliet's feet. "You don't have to check the radar," Juliet called. "It's me. And you don't have to arm any rockets, either!"

Granville's head appeared in the entrance to the fort. He was wearing his helmet. Black camouflage paint was streaked across his face. "Hold your fire!" he said. "It's friendly forces!"

"I'm not forces!" Juliet said. "Granville Jones, if you think I'm going to play war, I'm going home. I *hate* war. People get killed in wars."

Jonah stuck his head out of the fort. "Jeez, Juliet, it's just pretend," he said. His face was covered with paint as well, though he did not have a helmet.

"It's still scary," Juliet said. She folded her arms and glared up into the tree.

Jonah and Granville looked at each other. Jonah shrugged. "Okay, then," Granville said. "No war. The war's over. We're a peace-keeping force. We stand by the rocket launchers, but we don't use them. Now will you come up?"

Juliet surveyed the tree. The fort looked a long way up. Maybe ten feet in the air. "How?" she said.

"Just use the rungs that are nailed to the tree, until you get to the low branch," Granville said. "After that it's easy."

"Stay away from the pie tins on the ground, though," Jonah called. "They're land mines."

It didn't look easy to Juliet. It looked impossible. And there were pie tins scattered among the leaves on the ground around the tree.

For a moment, Juliet thought of home and her carpeted room at the top of the nice, solid stairs. Then she thought of her mother and the party invitations. She made her way past the pie tins and to the first rung on the tree.

By the third rung, Juliet was thinking about a parachute. It would be nice to have one. She reached the lowest branch of the tree. And then, without knowing quite how she managed it, she was in the tree fort.

Juliet took a deep breath. Her heart was pounding and her face felt hot. But she was no longer afraid. "I made it!" she said.

"See?" Granville said. "A piece of cake."

Juliet looked out the doorway of the fort. She could see rooftops all up and down the alley. She could even see a corner of her own roof.

"Do you need a drink?" Jonah asked. "We have some water right here." He pointed to a canteen hanging from a nail on one wall of the fort. Other nails held Granville's gas mask and walkie-talkie, a coiled rope with clothespins, a collection of rubber bands, a pair of binoculars with one lens missing, and a slingshot.

Juliet spotted a plastic bag full of seedpods from a liquidambar tree. "What are those for?" she asked.

"Those are grenades," Granville said. "Mostly, they're concussion grenades. They knock you out, but they don't kill you. Watch."

He took a seedpod from the bag and tossed it against the opposite wall. "Boom!" he yelled. Jonah fell over with his eyes closed. "Works good, huh?" Granville said.

"I told you," Juliet said. "I don't want to play war."

"I'm only knocked out," Jonah said.

"Yeah, no killing," Granville said. "He's still alive."

"I mean it," Juliet said.

Jonah opened his eyes. "You're no fun, Juliet," he said.

Juliet glared at him until he closed his eyes again. "If you want to know what I think," she said, "I think you could use this fort for something else."

"Such as?" Granville asked. He sounded suspicious.

"Such as something . . . well . . . nice," Juliet said. "Like it could be a castle bower. I could be the princess and you could each be a prince, coming to ask for my hand in marriage. The one with the best manners wins, of course."

"Oh, gross!" Granville said.

Jonah rolled on his side and made gagging noises.

"I'm going to radio for help," Granville said.

"Yeah, get reinforcements," Jonah said.

Juliet sniffed. "Well, it was just an idea," she said.

Granville spoke into the walkie-talkie. Juliet could hear his mother answering back from the kitchen. In a few minutes, Mrs. Jones arrived with a sackful of chocolate chip cookies. Granville lowered the rope, and Mrs.

Jones clipped the sack to the rope with the clothespins. Then Granville hauled it up. The cookies were homemade. Juliet supposed it would be all right to eat one. Or two or three.

It was a good while after the cookies, and after taking turns with the binoculars, and after watching Granville's cat, Mulberry, stalk a robin that Juliet remembered about the plan.

"It's a great plan," Jonah said. "Granville thought it up. But I helped."

"See, it goes like this," Granville said. "Mrs. Lacey put Lydia Jane next to you so you could set a good example, right?"

"Right," said Juliet.

"But Lydia Jane isn't following your example, right?"

"Right," said Juliet.

"So Lydia Jane is going to have to sit next to you forever," Granville said. "Right?"

"Right," Juliet said. She sighed. "So far this isn't sounding like much of a plan."

"We're just getting to the good part," Jonah said. "Wait."

"Yeah," Granville said. He leaned forward, his face only inches from Juliet's. "See, suppose instead of *you* rubbing off on Lydia Jane, Lydia Jane rubbed off on *you*?" He grinned a devilish grin. His eyes sparkled.

Juliet furrowed her brow. "I don't get it," she said.

"It's simple!" Jonah said. "It's foolproof! You'll start acting like Lydia Jane!"

Juliet gasped. "That could never happen!" she said.

"It could," Jonah said.

"If you *made* it," Granville said.

Juliet was suddenly feeling a little out of sorts. She leaned back against the wall of the fort and thought. "Even if I *wanted* to act like Lydia Jane," she said, "even if I *could*, I don't see how that would help. Then there'd just be one more person like Lydia Jane in the class. Mrs. Lacey wouldn't like that."

Jonah said something Juliet didn't quite catch. It sounded like "I would."

"You've got it!" Granville said to Juliet. He slapped his thigh. "When Mrs. Lacey sees that Lydia Jane rubbed off on you instead of the other way around, she'll have to send her back to her old seat!"

"If Lydia Jane rubbed off on me . . ." Juliet said, thinking. "Hmmmm," she said. Then she said it again, "Hmmmm . . ." For a time, she sat very still and said nothing. Then she said, "Wow."

Jonah and Granville laughed. "I told you it was great," Jonah said.

"It's more like a plot than a plan, though." A smile broke out around the corners of Juliet's mouth.

"Naturally," Granville said. He laughed again.

Juliet sat quietly for a bit, enjoying the plan. Then she had a troubling thought. "The only problem," she said, "is that I'm very used to being me. I'm not so sure I could get used to being someone else. Especially not someone like Lydia Jane Bly. She's so . . . well . . ."

"Fun!" Jonah said.

Juliet shot Jonah a look.

"Different?" Granville said.

"Different," she agreed. "Lydia Jane is very different."

"That's where we come in," Granville said. "We'll tell you what to do."

"You mean you're going to give me *orders*?" Juliet said.

"Yeah!" Jonah said.

"Not exactly orders," Granville said. "It's more like help. Pretend we're your trainers. Like if you were going to swim in the Olympics, you'd need a coach, right?"

"Well . . ." Juliet said. That didn't sound so bad. "Okay, I guess."

Granville picked up a seedpod grenade. He took the slingshot from its nail and zinged a shot across the yard. The pod hit the covered barbecue grille with a loud *pong*!

"Want a turn?" he asked Juliet.

"No, thanks," she said. "I don't like . . ."

"Try," Granville said. "Lydia Jane would."

For the rest of the morning, Juliet, Jonah, and Granville took turns with the slingshot. Juliet hit the barbecue only twice. But four times, she laughed out loud.

Jonah and Granville had lots of ideas for things Lydia Jane might do. Between turns with the slingshot, they told the ideas to Juliet.

Don't boss anybody around.

Don't announce people's mistakes.

Forget to do your homework.

Come late to school.

Say yes to everything.

"This sounds like a lot of work," Juliet said.

"You have to practice," Jonah said.

"Champions practice all the time," Granville said. "Even when you're alone, you have to practice."

At lunch time, Mrs. Jones brought out a basket of food. She tied it to the rope, and Granville hauled it carefully up.

"Egg salad on white bread," Juliet said. "I'm not supposed to eat eggs. My mother would kill me. And even the lemonade in that thermos is mostly sugar."

"Lydia Jane would love it," Jonah said.

"She'd gobble it up," Granville said.

"You mean this is training?" Juliet asked.

"Yes," Jonah and Granville said at once.

Juliet considered. "Well, if I'm going to be a champion . . ." And she *was* hungry. She poured lemonade into a paper cup.

After lunch, they practiced spying with the broken binoculars. They saw an orange tabby cat chase a leaf down the alley. Then they saw Granville's neighbor take out the trash.

Later, Granville radioed to his mother for his game of Battleship. Jonah and Granville played the first game. Then, even though it was about war, Juliet played against Jonah in the second. "Lydia Jane would," Granville said. Juliet wondered if Lydia Jane also would have lost.

Finally, Juliet knew it was time to go home.

And there was no getting out of it. She needed to use the bathroom.

"How would Lydia Jane get out of this tree?" she asked.

"She might jump," Granville said. "That's what I do."

"She might use a bungee cord and *then* jump," Jonah said. "That's what I'd do."

Juliet looked down at the ground. It was a lot farther away than it had been last time she'd looked. Maybe a hundred miles farther.

"Could the fire department fit their ladder truck in your backyard?" she asked. "I think I'm stuck."

"Come on," Granville said. "We'll help. You get down the same way you got up."

Jonah went ahead and guided Juliet to the right footholds. In no time, she was on the ground.

Granville climbed down to the lowest branch. Then he leaped with a yell, *"Hiiyyahhh!"*

Juliet squealed and jumped back.

"He does that," Jonah said. "Don't pay any attention."

Granville got to his feet and dusted himself off. "Remember," he said, "practice. Practice even when you're alone. You have to get good at this if the plan's going to work."

"I will," Juliet said. "I'm motivated."

Juliet walked down the alley toward home.

While she was walking, she thought it would be more like Lydia Jane to skip. So she did that.

Then she thought it would be just like Lydia Jane to skip right through a puddle.

So she did that, too.

Chapter 6

"I *don't know what's come over you lately,*" Mrs. Fisher said on Sunday. She and Juliet were buckled into the front seat of Mrs. Fisher's Dodge. "You tracked mud all the way through the kitchen yesterday.

"Then this morning you didn't make your bed," she went on, "even though I reminded you twice. And all that fuss you made about those invitations! They *still* wouldn't be mailed if I'd left it up to you."

"Well, you didn't," Juliet said. "So they're mailed." She turned and scowled out the window.

"And now you want to throw away money at Hooligan Hatchery, when the clothes at Bea's Young People's Shop are much nicer," her mother said.

"But Lyd . . . that is, *nobody* wears clothes from Bea's," Juliet said. "Except me."

Mrs. Fisher pulled up to the stoplight at Sierra Boulevard. She turned on her left turn signal. "Just because some people waste their money on shoddy goods doesn't mean we should," she said. "Bea's clothes are of the very best quality. And they're dignified. If you're going to be a doctor, you'll need to dress with dignity."

"I'll dress with dignity next year," Juliet said. "Right now, I need to dress with . . . zip."

"Zip!" The light changed and Mrs. Fisher turned the corner onto Sierra. "I never heard of such . . ."

"I'll pay for the clothes myself," Juliet said. "I have money in the bank."

"That's the money your grandmother sends you for Christmas and your birthday! I thought we agreed you'd save that for college."

"Well, college isn't *tomorrow*," Juliet said. "I have a little time."

Mrs. Fisher continued on down the highway. Her brow was furrowed. Juliet waited anxiously to see if her mother would turn in at the mall for Hooligan's, or continue on to the plaza where Bea's shop was.

At Westmont Mall, Mrs. Fisher flicked on her right-hand turn signal. Juliet sighed.

"Just this once," her mother said. "Before you need clothes again, we're going to have to come to an understanding. Is that clear?"

"It's clear," said Juliet.

Inside Hooligan Hatchery, Juliet tried on baggy pants and stretch pants. She tried on oversized T-shirts and Hawaiian flowered shirts. She tried on overalls and baseball caps and high-top sneakers. All the while, her mother watched and clucked her tongue. Sometimes she said, "Oh, my." Sometimes she sadly shook her head.

An hour later, Mrs. Fisher stood stiffly at the cashier's counter. Her checkbook was in her hand. "I can't believe I'm doing this," she muttered.

"Neither can I," Juliet muttered in return.

On the counter in front of them were a pair of baggy overalls, a pair of black stretch pants, and two extra-large T-shirts, one in neon green and the other a shocking pink with orange sleeves. There were two plastic snap-bracelets. There was one baseball cap. On the front was stitched, "National Turkey Week." And there was a pair of sneakers. Purple.

"These clothes are more than zippy," Mrs. Fisher said. "They're more than flashy, too. They're all the way to loud."

"I know," Juliet said. She tried to sound happy, but the truth was, she was worn out. It was a lot of work getting clothes that somebody else might wear. She wondered if Lydia Jane got this tired buying clothes for herself.

After Hooligan Hatchery, Mrs. Fisher stopped by The Paper Clip. She needed to buy three-by-five cards. She used the cards for copying recipes for healthy food. In the kitchen at home were three boxes of healthy recipes.

While her mother was in The Paper Clip, Juliet waited outside. One door down was the jewelry store. Juliet looked in the window of the jewelry store and thought about what kind of jewels a princess might wear. A princess would wear diamonds, she decided. Diamonds and gold.

A pair of diamond earrings caught Juliet's eye. Lydia Jane had earrings, Juliet recalled. Not diamonds, but small pink stones set in gold. And another pair. Frogs. Little green frogs with bug eyes.

Juliet fingered the lobe of one ear. "I wonder . . ." she said aloud.

Juliet and her mother were nearly home before Juliet asked her question. "Are you still going to buy me a birthday present?" she said. "After all these clothes, I mean."

"Why, yes," her mother said. "I don't mind buying your clothes, Juliet. It's *where* we buy them that concerns me."

"Would you like a hint, then?" Juliet asked.

"A hint about what?" her mother said. She was watching for cross traffic at the corner of Manzanita and Tehema.

"About what to get me for my birthday."

"Why, yes," her mother said. "I suppose that would be a help."

Juliet took a deep breath. She cleared her throat. "I want my ears pierced," she said at last.

"You *what*?" It was almost a yell.

"My ears," Juliet said. "Pierced."

"Well, that's the limit!" her mother said. "I never! Pierced ears, of all things! Juliet Fisher, you *know* how I feel about pierced ears on children."

"But Lyd . . . lots of kids have them," Juliet said.

"That is no earthly reason," her mother said. "You are not other kids, you're my daughter. And no daughter of mine is going to go poking holes in her body at the age of eight."

"I'll be nine on my birthday," Juliet reminded her.

"Nine then. Or ten," her mother said. "No. Absolutely not. No way." A car honked behind them, but Juliet's mother seemed not to hear.

Juliet slouched down in her seat. "It's just a couple of tiny holes," she said. "Tiny holes for tiny earrings."

"No!" her mother said again.

"And it's all I really want," Juliet persisted. "Just pierced ears, that's all. Well . . . that and maybe a can of mousse."

"Mousse!" her mother shrieked.

Several cars behind them honked at once. Mrs. Fisher stepped on the accelerator and they lurched forward.

At home, Juliet followed her mother into

the house. She had to race to keep up. Her mother was walking very fast.

"Talk to your daughter," she said to Mr. Fisher.

Juliet's father had been dozing on the couch with a book. He often dozed and read on Sundays. And he never watched TV. He said he had to look at things moving around on screens all day at work; why should he want to do it at home?

Mr. Fisher rubbed one eye. "What seems to be the trouble here?" he asked.

"I only said . . ." Juliet began.

"She's turned into a teenager!" her mother said. "Overnight! Did you ever hear of such a thing?

"First she insists on having all these . . . *noisy* clothes. And now, if you can imagine, she wants her ears pierced!"

Mrs. Fisher dropped her coat and purse on one of the wing chairs opposite the couch. She turned and stalked toward the kitchen. "You talk to her," she said. "She's *your* daughter. I have dinner to fix."

Juliet sank into the other wing chair. She clutched the handles of the shopping bag full of noisy clothes.

"Hmmmm," said Mr. Fisher. "I suppose you'd better tell me what's going on."

"It's just that I wanted to wear something different for a while," Juliet said.

"How different?" asked her father.

Juliet reached in the bag and pulled out the neon green T-shirt. She reached in with the other hand and held up a purple tennis shoe.

"Hmmmm," said her father again. "Very different." He stroked his unshaven chin with one hand. "And what exactly do you mean by a while?" he asked.

"A while," Juliet said. "It's temporary."

"Ah, well then," said Mr. Fisher, "as long as it's temporary." He picked up his book and settled back on the couch.

Juliet waited for a bit to see if the talking-to was over. Evidently it was. She picked up the shopping bag and went to her room.

She hoped that the rest of Granville's plan

was easier than the part about the clothes. Getting the clothes had been hard.

Getting her ears pierced would probably be impossible, Juliet decided. But then, that wasn't really part of the plan. Having her ears pierced was an idea Juliet had thought up entirely on her own.

Juliet took the tags off the new clothes and hung them in her closet. Then she went back and got some out. These she flung on her desk and chair. Lydia Jane probably flung her clothes all over, she thought.

She looked around her room for something else that Lydia Jane might do. She remembered what Granville had said: practice was important. She should practice even while she was alone.

Juliet bounced on her bed until her mother hollered up the stairs. Then she sat down at her desk, on her new clothes, and did exactly half of her math homework.

At the dinner table that night, Juliet put her elbows on the table. She didn't put her napkin in her lap.

"You see?" said Juliet's mother. "Overnight she's changed."

Mr. Fisher poked at a piece of steamed fish. "It's temporary," he said. "Don't get excited."

"That's very easy for you to say," Mrs. Fisher huffed. "I'm watching years of good training go down the drain, and you tell me not to get excited."

"Get excited if you like, then," said Juliet's father. "But I have to get to sleep. I have to be at work in a few hours." He carried his empty plate to the sink, tousled Juliet's hair, and went to bed.

Juliet waited until her mother turned on the dishwasher. Then she went to the living room to make a phone call. She needed to talk to Granville.

"Are you sure this is going to work?" she said to him.

"Sure," Granville said. "If you practice, that is. Have you been practicing?"

Juliet told him about tracking in the mud, bouncing on her unmade bed, leaving half her homework undone, and using bad table manners. "Is that enough?" she asked.

"For now," Granville said. "But practice more tomorrow."

"Well . . ." Juliet said, "I will. But I'm getting worried. My mother is mad. And I think my parents had a quarrel. It was a little hard to tell, because usually they only quarrel on Saturdays."

"Mine quarrel on any old day," Granville said. "But they always make up."

Juliet told him about the clothes. And she told him her idea about pierced ears.

"Great," he said. "Good thinking, Juliet."

"It may be a great idea," Juliet said, "but I don't think my mother will ever let me have my ears pierced. She hit the roof."

"Juliet," Granville said, "it's a good thing you have me for a coach. I don't think you understand parents very well."

"I don't?" Juliet said.

"No. See, if you want pierced ears, you don't *ask* to have your ears pierced."

"I don't?" Juliet said again. "Then what . . ."

"You ask to have your *nose* pierced. Then your mother will suggest you have your ears pierced all by herself."

"Ohhhh," Juliet said. She was beginning to see. And it might just be true what people said about Granville—he really was a genius!

"See you tomorrow," he said.

"You'll see *some*body tomorrow," Juliet said. "I'm just not sure it'll be me."

Chapter 7

On Monday morning, three people spoke to Juliet as she entered the class.

Amber Arlington said, "Juliet?"

Kenny Ota said, "Whoa, Juliet!"

Mindy Rufkin said, "Quality duds, Juliet."

From their desks across the room, Jonah and Granville waved two thumbs up.

Lydia Jane came in just at the end of sharing. "I know, I know, I'm late again," she said.

Juliet shrugged. "I'm probably going to be late tomorrow," she said.

Mrs. Lacey put the spelling words on the board. *Often, handle, mopped, goat, paint, hasty, thorn, bear, noon, sight.* "Copy the words from the board," she said. "Write each word in a sentence. If you don't have time to finish today, you'll have more time on Wednesday."

Juliet and Lydia Jane each got out a piece of paper. Lydia Jane's was smudged and ragged. Juliet's was crisp and new. Juliet wadded her paper into a tight ball, then smoothed it out again.

Lydia Jane copied the spelling words onto her paper. Juliet did the same. Lydia Jane numbered her paper from one to three with wide spaces between the numbers.

Juliet wrote the number one. She wrote it very large. Then she thought for a long time. Finally she wrote:

At noon the hasty boy couldn't wait

for lunch, so he ran barefoot across the barnyard and pretty often he stepped on a thorn on the way, or knocked over a bucket of paint, and then grabbed the goat, and used its tail for a handle and mopped the whole mess up, which was a sight too silly to bear.

"Whew!" Juliet said. "Ten at one blow."

Lydia Jane leaned over to look at Juliet's paper. "You fit them all in one sentence!" she said. "I'm going to try that next time."

"I'll probably get a D," Juliet said.

"Probably," Lydia Jane agreed. They both smiled.

On Tuesday morning, Juliet was late to school. She arrived just after Lydia Jane.

"Cool shirt," Lydia Jane said.

"Thanks," said Juliet.

"I have one almost like it," Lydia Jane said. "Except mine has a fuchsia stripe around the bottom."

"I know," Juliet said.

"Of course, it's faded now," Lydia Jane said. "And it has stains. A grass stain on the shoulder. And some juice."

"This one will have stains soon," Juliet said. "Maybe tomorrow."

At math time, Juliet and Lydia Jane drew mazes around the edge of page fifty-three in their workbooks. Then they traded books and worked each other's mazes.

"I have raccoons under my house," Lydia Jane said. "I can hear them at night. They have fights and snarl. Or maybe that's just how they talk. I'm trying to figure it out. I'm hoping maybe they'll have babies this spring.

"They knock over the trash in the night," she went on. "Then they take the garbage down to the creek and wash it before they eat it. *I* wouldn't eat it even if I washed it first. But I guess they know what they're doing.

"Raccoons are nocturnal," Lydia Jane said. "Did you know that? Nocturnal means they sleep in the day and stay awake at night. I'd like to be nocturnal. Then I could stay up and watch Jay Leno on TV. Want to try being nocturnal with me?"

"Sure," Juliet said.

Lydia Jane laid her head on the desk and closed her eyes. Juliet did the same.

On Wednesday, it rained again. Juliet and Lydia Jane ate lunch at their desks. Juliet had low-fat cottage cheese, a banana, celery sticks, low-salt V-8 juice, and a carob bar. Lydia Jane had a bologna sandwich on white, corn chips, root beer, and two cupcakes in a cellophane pack.

"Cottage cheese is good on corn chips," Lydia Jane said. "Want some?"

"Sure," Juliet said.

Lydia Jane dumped a pile of corn chips on Juliet's desk. Juliet shared the cottage cheese with Lydia Jane. They split the bologna sandwich and the banana. They shared the cupcakes. They threw the carob bar in the trash.

On Thursday afternoon, the class worked on the habitat studies. Juliet took her pictures of locks and cleansers and containers across the room and dropped them in the trash can. She glued the photo of Canyon de Chelly on a piece of paper. Under it she wrote, "You can go here when you have a bad day. When things improve, you can come back." Then she cut out pictures of playground equipment.

Lydia Jane worked on a drawing of a small, furry animal with a long snout. "It's a shrew," she said. "A shrew is sort of like a mole, but not quite.

"Shrews eat lots of insects. They eat their own weight in insects every three hours. My habitat is going to have lots of shrews. That way the farmers won't need pesticides. And the Earth won't get poisoned. And birds can lay eggs with strong shells. The way I see it, shrews are the answer to nearly everything.

"The best part is that other animals won't eat them up," Lydia Jane said. "Know why?

Because they stink." She drew fume lines rising from the shrew.

"I'm making a playground for old people," Juliet said. "I'm going to have escalators going up to the tops of the slides. And the swings will be motorized. The monkey bars will be over two feet of soft foam. There'll be a merry-go-round, and all the horses will be sidesaddle."

Juliet smeared rubber cement on a piece of paper. She slapped down a picture of a slide and another of a merry-go-round. Glue oozed from the edges of the pictures. Juliet rubbed at it with her hand. Then she wiped her hand on her shirt.

At the end of school on Friday, Juliet put on her National Turkey Week cap and raced out the door. Jonah and Granville were waiting for her. They were going to Juliet's to pick up a container of vegetarian goulash. Then they were going to visit Mr. Rosetti.

"You're doing great," Granville said as they walked across the playing field toward home.

"Totally awesome."

"It's amazing," Jonah said. "Sometimes I can't tell you and Lydia Jane apart."

Juliet beamed with pride.

"Think you can keep it up?" Granville asked.

"I think so," Juliet said. "It was hard at first. I had to concentrate all the time to think of what Lydia Jane would do. And I kept thinking someone would kill me. But once you get used to it, it's really pretty easy."

Then she remembered something. "The only thing is, if I have to do this for very long, I'm going to get a rotten report card. Do you think it'll work soon?"

"Bound to," Jonah said.

"Sure thing," Granville said. "It might be working already."

"Really?" Juliet said. "How can you tell?"

"We've seen Mrs. Lacey looking at you," Granville said.

"Yeah," Jonah said. "Like when you went

to sleep on your desk. She looked about six times!"

"Wow!" Juliet said.

"And when you and Lydia Jane were talking during Silent Reading. She looked then, too."

They crossed the street and headed down Manzanita.

"Then it must be working," Juliet agreed. "How did she look? Did she look mad?"

"Well . . ." Jonah said.

"More like *interested*," Granville said.

Juliet considered. "Mad would be better," she said. "Don't you think it would work better if she was getting mad? My mother is getting pretty mad, I know that."

"Oh, but interested is good," Granville said.

"Yeah," Jonah said. "Mrs. Lacey isn't really the mad type, if you know what I mean."

"I guess that's right . . ." Juliet said.

"Mothers get mad," Granville said.

"Teachers get interested. But it's the same thing."

Juliet thought this over. She decided it made sense. "So it'll work soon, huh?" she said.

"I think so," Jonah said.

"Yeah," Granville said. "I'm pretty sure."

"That's good," Juliet said. "Because yesterday my mother was talking about selling me. Cheap."

While Jonah and Granville waited outside, Juliet went in through the back door of her house to the kitchen. She dropped her backpack on the floor near the stairs to her room. Then she got the plastic container of goulash from the refrigerator.

"Mind your manners at Mr. Rosetti's," her mother said. "And don't slam the door; your father's sleeping."

That wouldn't stop Lydia Jane, Juliet said to herself. She pulled the back door to, then let the screen door go with a bang.

Jonah, Granville, and Juliet stopped by

Granville's house. Jonah and Granville dropped their backpacks on Granville's front porch. Granville ran inside and came back with both his walkie-talkies. Then all three cut across the lawn to Mr. Rosetti's house.

"Well, what have we here?" Mr. Rosetti said when he came to the door. "I recognize these two young men, but I don't believe I've met this young woman."

"Yes, you have," Juliet told him. "It's me. Juliet."

"Juliet *Fisher*?" Mr. Rosetti said. "No, it can't be. You must be another Juliet."

Juliet handed the goulash to Granville and pulled off her cap. "See?" she said.

"Well, so it is," Mr. Rosetti said. "In that case, do come in."

Juliet noticed that Jonah was trying to keep a straight face. So was Granville, for that matter.

"You knew all along," she said to Mr. Rosetti.

"Well," he said, as he ushered them inside, "I do admit I'd heard something. Your mother phoned me to say she was sending this goulash. She might have mentioned something about you then." His eyes were twinkling.

"The goulash has bean curd in it," Juliet said. "Not everybody likes bean curd."

"Yech," Granville said.

"I'm sure it will be very good," Mr. Rosetti said. "I'll just put it in the refrigerator for now." He took the container of goulash and headed toward the kitchen.

"Hey," Jonah said. "No cane! Is your hip all better, Mr. Rosetti?"

"Just about," Mr. Rosetti said. "I still use the cane if I go out in the yard. But just about."

Mr. Rosetti's kitten scampered in from the dining room. It came to a sliding stop near Mr. Rosetti's feet.

Mr. Rosetti set the goulash on the counter and bent to pick up the kitten. He scratched it under the chin. "Jonah," he said, "Granville, Juliet, I'd like to introduce you to Walter."

"Walter?" Granville said.

"Walter's a person's name," said Jonah.

"Well, now," Mr. Rosetti said, as he stroked the kitten, "that's the interesting thing. You see, this kitten likes to follow me around, so for a while I thought a dog's name might be best, after all. But then I noticed I talk to this kitten a great deal. I thought I'd feel a little foolish if I found myself saying, 'Now, imagine that, Rover.' I decided I'd feel more comfortable talking to someone named Walter than someone named Rover. So, this is Walter."

"Makes sense," Jonah said.

Mr. Rosetti handed the kitten to Jonah while he put the goulash away. Then he got out some grape juice and served a cup to each of them. Juliet stuck a finger in the juice and dabbed a few drops down the front of her shirt.

"My mother says you'd like to take a walk around the block," Jonah said. "We thought we could go with you. We could make sure you were safe on the way."

"Wonderful!" Mr. Rosetti said. "It's been weeks since I've been farther than the edge of this property. I'd like nothing better."

Jonah, Granville, Juliet, and Mr. Rosetti made a procession down the sidewalk. Granville went twenty yards ahead. Jonah walked twenty yards behind. They watched for booby traps, land mines, and sneak attacks by the enemy. They also watched for kids on skateboards or roller skates. They radioed back and forth.

"Advance guard clear. Over."

"Rear guard clear."

Juliet walked beside Mr. Rosetti. She figured if he started to fall she could make a grab for him.

"Your mother's sounding a little . . . frazzled," Mr. Rosetti said. "She mentioned something about a ring for your nose."

"Well . . ." Juliet said, "I did ask her if I could have my nose pierced. Some people do, you know."

"Oh, I know," Mr. Rosetti said. "Of course, it's none of my business, and nobody asked my advice, but I'd recommend a compromise. Maybe you could have your ears pierced instead, and save the nose for later. I do see girls your age with pierced ears."

"Good idea!" Juliet said. "My mother could even make it a birthday present. Maybe you could suggest that to her."

"Oh, I already did," Mr. Rosetti said. "I wouldn't say she was eager, exactly. But I would say she seemed to warm to the idea."

"Oh, great!" Juliet said. She gave a little skip. Then, without actually thinking about it, she took hold of Mr. Rosetti's free hand.

"You know, Juliet," said Mr. Rosetti, "when I first met you, you reminded me a little of my sister, Violet. But not today. What has brought about this change in you? If you don't mind my asking, that is."

"I don't mind," Juliet said. "It's just that it's a little hard to explain. It's like an experiment, only different. But don't worry, it's temporary."

"Temporary?" Mr. Rosetti said. "Well, to tell the truth, I'm a little sorry to hear that, Juliet. I was rather enjoying the new you."

Juliet sighed. "To tell the truth," she said, "so was I."

They walked along in silence for a few minutes. Then Juliet said, "One thing I've noticed—since I've been just like Lyd . . . like *this*, kids talk to me more. Lydia Jane even said she was coming to my birthday party. And three other kids said they might."

"Well, temporary can mean all kinds of things," Mr. Rosetti said. "I worked in a temporary office building for twenty-three years."

Juliet thought. "We have some temporary classrooms at our school," she said. "They've been there ever since I was in kindergarten."

"So you see . . ." Mr. Rosetti said.

"So I see," Juliet said.

They both laughed.

Chapter 8

Juliet knew the day had finally come. It was Thursday afternoon, two days before Juliet's birthday. It was the day Mrs. Lacey would move Lydia Jane back to her old seat.

The completed habitat studies sat in a pile on Mrs. Lacey's desk. Juliet could see that hers was on top. Twice during the morning, Mrs. Lacey had opened Juliet's habitat report and leafed through the pages. Twice she had closed it and looked at Juliet. The look was very interested.

Mrs. Lacey had looked at Juliet again during noon recess. Juliet was playing kickball for the third day in a row. It was three days more than she had ever played kickball before.

Lydia Jane always played kickball. "Don't just wait at home plate for the ball to get to you," she said to Juliet. "Stand behind the plate and run towards the ball when it's pitched. It'll go much farther that way."

Juliet did as Lydia Jane suggested. She kicked two balls into left field.

"You need to learn to slide," Lydia Jane said. "If someone throws the ball when you're running to a base, just slide. Try it."

She showed Juliet how to bend one knee. She showed her how to keep her arm out of the way. The next time Juliet was up, she slid into first base.

Juliet brushed herself off and twisted to see the seat of her baggy overalls. They were grass-stained from hip to ankle. "Yes!" she said.

"All right!" Lydia Jane yelled.

That's when Juliet noticed Mrs. Lacey looking at her again. Mrs. Lacey's look was even more interested than it had been before. It was *very* interested.

When Lydia Jane's turn came, she kicked a home run. She kicked it so far into right field that nobody even bothered to chase it. Then she danced around the bases. She skipped and hopped and blew kisses. When she got to home plate she took a bow. Everyone laughed and cheered.

If I ever get a home run, Juliet decided, I'm going to dance around the bases just like Lydia Jane.

For the rest of the day, Juliet and Lydia Jane chattered in class. And for the rest of the day, every time Juliet looked at Mrs. Lacey, Mrs. Lacey was looking at her. With interest.

"I might be getting my ears pierced," Juliet

said. "My mother asked at the hospital, and it turns out four doctors had kids my age with pierced ears. So my mother says it might be okay."

"Cool," Lydia Jane said. "Try for two holes in each ear. That's what I want. Then I could wear four different earrings at once." She turned her head so that Juliet could see both ears. She had a frog in one and a pink stone in the other.

"I was hoping for diamonds," Juliet said. "But the fake kind. They cost hardly anything."

"I want stars next," Lydia Jane said. "But the fake kind of those, too."

She tore the eraser off a pencil and dropped it on the desk in front of Juliet. "Pretend that's a neutron star and pick it up," she said.

Juliet reached for the eraser.

"But you *can't* pick it up," Lydia Jane said quickly. "A neutron star that big would weigh too much to pick up. It would weigh millions of tons. In fact, it would be so heavy it wouldn't be here at all. It would fall through the desk. It would fall through the floor. It would probably fall through the whole Earth!"

"Wow!" Juliet said.

"So that's why fake stars make better earrings," Lydia Jane said. "Try it if you don't believe me."

Granville detoured by Juliet's seat on the way to the pencil sharpener. He whispered in Juliet's ear, "Have you seen Mrs. Lacey? I think our plan worked!" He clapped Juliet on the back.

Juliet nodded. She thought Granville was right. Then she had another thought. When Mrs. Lacey moves Lydia Jane's seat, I might miss her.

It was nearly time for the bell when Mrs. Lacey touched Juliet on the shoulder. She said, "If you could spare a few minutes after school, I'd like a word with you."

Juliet packed her notebook and sat quietly

in her seat while the other children filed out. She was suddenly uncertain and confused. What if Mrs. Lacey got angry like her mother had? What if she said, "Shape up right now, kid." Juliet knew she was supposed to say something about Lydia Jane. But what? She wished Granville would come back and help with this part of the plan.

Mrs. Lacey slid into the seat next to Juliet. In her hand was the habitat report. She set it on the desk and opened it to the middle.

"This is not like any of your other work this year," Mrs. Lacey said.

Juliet stared at the open page. It was rimmed with smears of rubber cement and grimy fingerprints. "I know," she said. "It's messy."

"Is it?" Mrs. Lacey said. "I hadn't noticed. What caught my attention was these two people. I wonder if you could tell me more about them?"

"Well . . ." Juliet said. She leaned forward

and pointed to the figure on the left-hand page. "This is the person in the regular army. He's wearing battle fatigues. I found that picture in a news magazine. It's also where I found the picture of the rocket launcher and the tank."

"Mmmmm," Mrs. Lacey said.

Juliet pointed to the figure on the right-hand page. "I found this picture in a fashion magazine," she said. "This person is in the Farmy Army. This will be the Farmy Army uniform. Orange parachute pants, a white T-shirt, rainbow suspenders, and a big green leaf in the middle of the shirt. I had to add the leaf."

"I see that," Mrs. Lacey said.

"The Farmy Army people have all these shiny tools," Juliet went on. "In my habitat, you get paid the same amount of money to be in the Farmy Army as you do in the regular army. But the Farmy Army people go all over the world and help poor people grow food. Anyone who didn't want to get killed in a war could be in the Farmy Army instead. Plus, there'd be less wars if everyone had enough to eat."

"Ahhhh," Mrs. Lacey said. She thoughtfully rubbed her jaw. "Now tell me, Juliet, where did you get the idea for this Farmy Army?"

"I think I got it from Granville," Juliet said. "See, Granville wears all this army stuff. But I don't think he really wants to kill anyone. I think he just likes the equipment. And the uniform. So I had the idea that if there was a good uniform and equipment to help keep people *alive* instead of killing them, lots of people would do that instead . . ." She caught her breath. None of this had anything to do with Lydia Jane.

"And what is this?" Mrs. Lacey asked. She pointed to a bowl and a spray of bright colors in the corner of the page.

"Oh, that's the popcorn and fireworks," Juliet said. "In the Farmy Army you can have those every week. It's for people who like to see things explode, but don't like to see people get hurt."

Mrs. Lacey leaned back in her chair. "Wonderful," she said. "Absolutely wonderful." She looked like she'd just eaten a big bowl of ice cream.

"You mean I'm not going to get an F?" Juliet asked. "It's pretty messy."

"An F!" Mrs. Lacey said. "Why, Juliet, this is the best work you've done all year. It's so . . . imaginative. This is A work! But I do wish you'd write a paragraph or two explaining what you just told me about the Farmy Army."

Juliet waited for the part about Lydia Jane. But Mrs. Lacey only sat quietly, gazing at the person in the Farmy Army uniform.

Finally, Juliet said, "Is there something else you wanted to say to me?"

"Huh?" Mrs. Lacey said. Then, "Oh, no, you may leave now, Juliet, thank you." Then, "Oh, except that I did want to tell you that I saw you slide into first base today. Very impressive. Very, very impressive, Juliet."

"You aren't going to move Lydia Jane's seat?" Juliet asked.

"Lydia Jane's seat?" Mrs. Lacey said. "I wouldn't dream of it! Whyever would you think that?"

Juliet tugged at the sleeve of her shirt. She was more confused than ever now. "Because of my homework," she said. "And because of my spelling and because Lydia Jane and I do nothing but talk all day."

"Oh, you do *something* besides talk." Mrs. Lacey picked up Juliet's habitat report and smiled at it fondly.

"And because I was supposed to set a good example, but Lydia Jane rubbed off on me instead," Juliet finished.

Mrs. Lacey blinked. "Set an example?" she said. "Goodness, Juliet, having you set an example was the farthest thing from my mind!"

Now it was Juliet's turn to blink. "Then what . . . ?"

"Oh, dear," Mrs. Lacey said, more to herself than Juliet, "what a muddle. But, yes, I can see how a person might think . . ."

She turned to Juliet. "You see, Juliet," she said, "your work has always been the best in this class. And except for a tendency to point out other people's mistakes, your behavior has been the best, too. I was just worried that you weren't having much fun. And I thought perhaps sitting next to Lydia Jane would remedy that."

"You wanted me to have *fun*?" Juliet asked. This talk with Mrs. Lacey was nothing like what she'd expected.

"Well, I don't believe that learning needs to be drudgery," Mrs. Lacey said. "And you are having fun, aren't you? Oh, I do hope so."

"Well," Juliet said, "I guess I am. That is, probably." She hesitated for a moment. "It's just that I'm not very used to having fun, Mrs. Lacey, so sometimes it's a little hard to tell."

"Then keep at it," Mrs. Lacey said. "It will soon feel natural."

Juliet walked out into the sunlight of the spring afternoon. In her mind, she tried to sort out what had been a plan and what had not been a plan. And what had gone wrong and what had gone right. It was very mixed up.

All she knew for sure was that Lydia Jane's seat would not be moved. Juliet thought about this, and then she sighed. It was a sigh of relief.

And then, on the way home, she skipped. She didn't skip because Lydia Jane would. She skipped because she felt like it.

Chapter 9

On Saturday, the morning of Juliet's birth-day, Mr. Fisher stood peering into the kitchen garbage pail.

"What are all these eggshells doing in here?" he asked.

"They're from my cake," Juliet said.

"Six eggs in one cake?" Mr. Fisher said.

"It's a special day," Juliet's mother said. "And Juliet is only nine years old. She can afford to eat the occasional egg."

"Six eggs is not 'the occasional egg,' " Mr.

Fisher said. "Six eggs is a feast. Do you do this on my birthday?"

"No," Mrs. Fisher said. "Your cake I make with yeast."

Mr. Fisher let the lid drop on the garbage pail. "As I suspected," he said.

At eleven o'clock, Juliet's mother took her to Westmont Mall to have her ears pierced.

"I only ask one thing," Mrs. Fisher said on the way. "I want you to wait until you're twenty-four to have your nose pierced."

"Okay," Juliet said. "I can do that."

"Maybe by then you'll have outgrown the urge," her mother said.

"And one more thing. I'd like you to keep up with your homework."

"I could do that," Juliet said.

"And I'd like you to put your clothes in the hamper sometimes," her mother went on.

"I could do that, too," Juliet said.

"And mind your table manners, please."

"Well . . ." Juliet said, "I could do that *some*times. But definitely not during my party."

"And another thing . . ."

"How many pairs of earrings are you buying me?" Juliet asked.

"Just one," her mother said.

"Then that's enough things," Juliet said.

By two o'clock, Juliet had two new holes in her ears. And two earrings. Fake diamond. She was dressed in her noisiest clothes and ready for guests.

"Couldn't you have worn a dress?" her mother asked. "You have so many pretty dresses."

"If I did that, everyone would go home," Juliet said.

"It's not the clothes that count," her mother said. "It's the person inside them."

"I think that's what she means," her father said. When the doorbell rang, he said, "Call me when the cake is served." He put his earplugs in his ears and went to his room.

Jonah and Granville arrived first. They were carrying one large package and one small one.

"We don't usually go to girls' parties," Granville said.

"We made an exception," Jonah said.

"And if you play musical chairs, we're leaving."

Juliet put her hands on her hips. "Do I look like someone who would play musical chairs?" she asked.

"Well . . ." Jonah said. He looked at Granville.

"Not as much as you used to," Granville said. He thrust the large package into Juliet's hands.

"This feels empty," Juliet said.

"Open it!" Jonah said.

Juliet took the package to the sofa and sat down. She carefully untied the ribbon. Then she tore off the paper. She lifted the lid of the box.

"It *is* empty!" she said.

"We thought you'd say that," Jonah said.

"See, it's not really empty," Granville said. "It's one free plan, from me and Jonah.

We didn't know how else to wrap it."

"It's a *big* plan," Jonah said. "It needed a big box."

Juliet laughed. "Maybe if you'd wrapped the last plan, it would have worked better," she said.

"It worked great!" Jonah said.

"Terrific!" Granville agreed. "It was our best plan yet."

In the other box was one walkie-talkie unit. Jonah and Granville said it was so Juliet could call them at the fort.

"It's on our frequency," Granville said.

"Call any time," Jonah said. "Or just come to the tree fort and yell up."

Mindy and Amber came to the party, along with two other girls from the class. And Mr. Rosetti came. He came by himself, using his cane.

"Your mother has my gift for you," Mr. Rosetti said. "It's hidden in a cupboard, I believe."

Mrs. Fisher disappeared into the kitchen.

In a minute, she came back carrying a small, rectangular glass tank. In it was a fish. A bright blue fish with long, flowing fins.

"It's a betta," Mr. Rosetti said, "sometimes known as a Siamese fighting fish. I thought it might be a good pet for someone who has allergies."

Everyone crowded around as the fish darted from one side of the tank to another.

"It's beautiful," Juliet said. "I could watch it forever."

"I was hoping you'd like it," Mr. Rosetti said. "But do be careful to keep the tank away from mirrors. Siamese fighting fish have been known to fight their own reflections."

"Weird," Jonah said.

"Dumb," Granville said.

"Well, yes and no," Mr. Rosetti said. "If you think about it, people sometimes do the same thing."

Finally, Lydia Jane arrived. Late. She gave

Juliet a can of mousse. And one earring. It was a star. Fake.

"I have the other one," Lydia Jane said. "We can wear them on the same day. And mousse is good if you want to have hair with *attitude*."

"That's just what I want," Juliet said. "I think my hair could use an attitude."

Juliet's mother groaned.

Juliet and her guests played ring toss and freeze tag. They had a scavenger hunt. Everyone won prizes. The prizes were water snakes.

"They'll squirt water from twenty paces," Juliet explained. "You can shoot and nobody gets hurt. I picked them myself."

"Awesome," Granville said. He spritzed Juliet right in the neck.

Juliet spritzed him back. "You're right," she said. "It's awesome." She spritzed him again.

Later, Lydia Jane said, "Your room is cool. I could come spend the night sometime. I could bring my flashlight. I have cards I can put over the lens to show constellations. We could shine constellations on your ceiling. I also tell great ghost stories. They'll make you scream."

"Or maybe we could play castle," Juliet said. "My room would work good for a castle. You could be the prince. Or I'd let you be the princess if you want."

Lydia Jane wrinkled her nose. "I'd rather be a wizard," she said. "Wizards can do magic. They can even make people disappear. I'd like to learn to do that."

"It won't work," Juliet said. "I've tried it. I tried to make *you* disappear, believe it or not."

Lydia Jane grinned a mischievous grin. She picked up one of the pointed party hats from the table and put it on. "That's why it didn't work then," she said. "It's because I'm the wizard. The wizard *never* disappears, Juliet. You should know that."

Juliet looked at the hat. Then she looked

at Lydia Jane. The hat looked just like a wizard's hat, Juliet decided. And it exactly suited Lydia Jane.

"You're right," Juliet said. "The wizard *shouldn't* disappear. I know that now."

Natalie Honeycutt says, "Once in a great while, a character pops to mind fully developed and ready to take his or her place in a book . . . sometimes to take over. Lydia Jane did this, and I love her for it."

Ms. Honeycutt is also the author of *Invisible Lissa* and two other books about Jonah and his classmates, *The Best-Laid Plans of Jonah Twist* and *The All New Jonah Twist* (all Bradbury Press). *Publishers Weekly* called *The All New Jonah Twist* a "winner . . . full of delightful surprises," and *Kirkus Reviews* commented, "a humorous, compassionate story that's right on target." *The Best-Laid Plans of Jonah Twist* was praised as "an excellent choice for independent readers [that] will also become a favorite read-aloud for younger children" (*School Library Journal*).

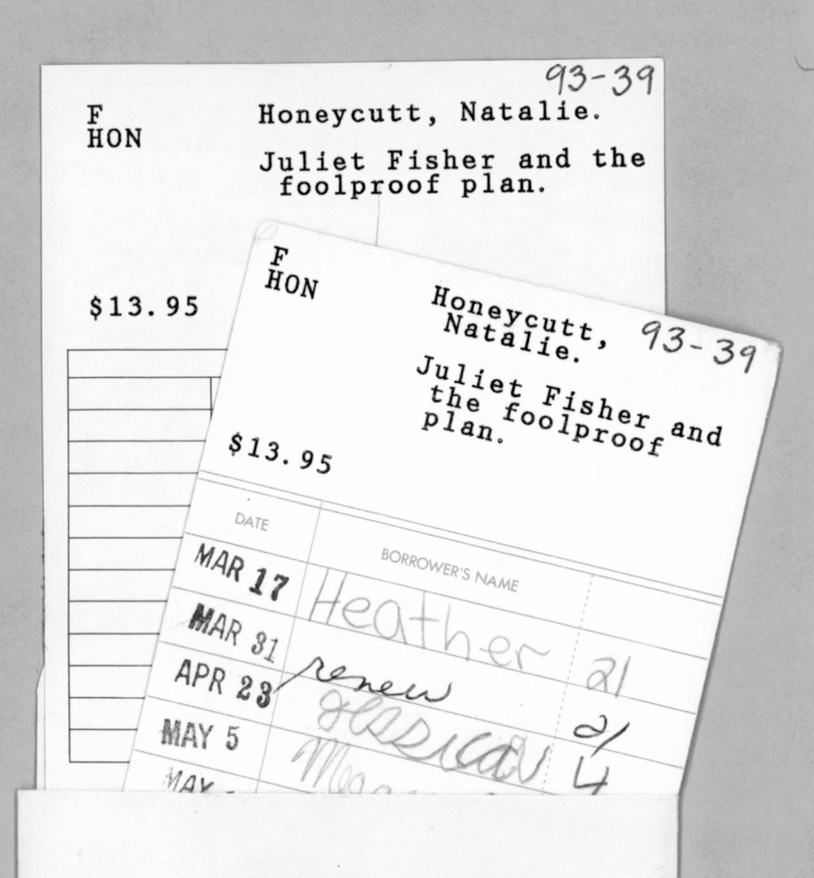
93-39
F
HON
Honeycutt, Natalie.
Juliet Fisher and the foolproof plan.
$13.95
F
HON
Honeycutt, Natalie.
93-39
Juliet Fisher and the foolproof plan.
$13.95
DATE
BORROWER'S NAME
MAR 17
Heather
MAR 31
renew
21
APR 23
MAY 5
21
4